UNUS★★ ★ DAY ★

SANDI TOKSVIG
Illustrated by Georgien Overwater

www.kidsatrandomhouse.co.uk

To Jesse, Meg and Bear

Also available in COLOUR FIRST READER books:

THE MONSTER CRISP-GUZZLER *by Malorie Blackman*
THE GHOST TEACHER *by Tony Bradman*
HAPPY MOUSEDAY *by Dick King-Smith*
TOO BIG! *by Geraldine McCaughrean*
INVISIBLE VINNIE *by Jenny Nimmo*
THE DINOSAUR'S PACKED LUNCH *by Jacqueline Wilson*
THE MONSTER STORY-TELLER *by Jacqueline Wilson*

UNUSUAL DAY
A CORGI BOOK 978 0 552 56583 7

Published in Great Britain by Corgi Books,
an imprint of Random House Children's Books
A Random House Group Company

Corgi Pups edition published 1997
This Colour First Reader edition published 2012

1 3 5 6 9 10 8 6 4 2

Text copyright © Sandi Toksvig, 1997
Illustrations copyright © Georgien Overwater, 1997

The right of Sandi Toksvig to be identified as the author of this work
has been asserted in accordance with the Copyright, Designs and Patents Act 1988.

Set in Bembo MT Schoolbook

Corgi Books are published by Random House Children's Books,
61–63 Uxbridge Road, London W5 5SA

www.**kids**at**randomhouse**.co.uk
www.**totallyrandombooks**.co.uk
www.**randomhouse**.co.uk

Addresses for companies within The Random House Group Limited
can be found at: www.randomhouse.co.uk/offices.htm

THE RANDOM HOUSE GROUP Limited Reg. No. 954009

A CIP catalogue record for this book is available from the British Library.

Printed in China

The Random House Group Limited supports The Forest Stewardship Council (FSC®), the leading international
forest certification organisation. Our books carrying the FSC label are printed on FSC® certified paper. FSC is
the only forest certification scheme endorsed by the leading environmental organisations, including Greenpeace.
Our paper procurement policy can be found at www.randomhouse.co.uk/environment

MIX
Paper from
responsible sources
FSC
www.fsc.org   FSC® C020056

CONTENTS

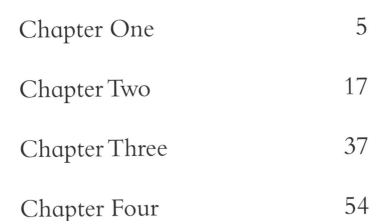

COLOUR FIRST READER books are perfect for beginner readers. All the text inside this Colour First Reader book has been checked and approved by a reading specialist, so it is the ideal size, length and level for children learning to read.

Series Reading Consultant: Prue Goodwin
Reading and Language Information Centre,
University of Reading

Chapter One

Blue Class were having an 'Unusual Day'. Well, there was nothing unusual about the day itself. Everyone had been to assembly as usual, everyone had done quiet reading as usual and everyone had drunk their juice in break as usual. It was after lunch that the unusual part was to happen.

All the children had been asked
to bring in something 'unusual'
to talk about. The idea had
started with Blue Class having a
'Blue Day' where everyone had
to bring in something blue.

Then they had had a 'Nature Day' where everyone had to bring something from the garden, followed by 'Pet Day'. 'Pet Day' had not been entirely successful. All the dogs, cats and hamsters had behaved very well, but

Kristian's snake had gone missing.
The classroom had been turned
upside down looking for Barry
the Boa.

9

The snake finally turned up ten
minutes before the bell in the
Rainy Day Box. Mrs Robinson,
who played piano on Tuesdays,
had found him. It was a shame
Barry had given her such a fright,

but everyone had had such fun
playing hospital while they
waited for her to come round.
Blue Class's teacher, Miss Johnson,
who has very red hair and is in
charge, says there won't be music
on Tuesdays this term.

Today, however, was 'Unusual Day'. Miss Johnson had told the children they could bring in anything that was really different. Joey had brought a doll from Russia called a 'Babushka'.

It was made of brightly painted
wood and had lots of other dolls
inside it. Kristian had brought a
nappy from his baby sister. She
had worn it all night and it was
still dry. His mother had said it
was 'most unusual'. Esme, who
had been a big hit on 'Nature

13

Day' with her slug collection, had found a four-leafed clover.

As they arrived, everyone had put their unusual things on the big table so that Miss Johnson

could label them. Jessica Grace
was late.

"Hello Jessica," said Miss
Johnson, putting someone's three-
legged *My Little Pony* at the back
of the table. "Have you brought
something unusual today?"

"Yes," said Jessica. "She's outside."

"She?" asked Miss Johnson.
Jessica nodded. "I've brought
my granny."

Chapter Two

"Your granny?" Miss Johnson looked down at Jessica. "I don't think you've understood, Jessica. Today is 'Unusual Day'. You were supposed to bring

something different. Something
unusual. 'Family Day' isn't until
next week. You can bring Granny
on 'Family Day'."

Just then Jessica's granny came
into the room. Jessica's granny

looked quite like a granny. She had grey hair like a granny and lines on her face like a granny. She did have a tracksuit and trainers on, but other than that Miss Johnson really didn't think she looked unusual at all.

Anyway, all the unusual things
were supposed to go on the big
table and have a label put on
them. It was a bit difficult
to put a granny in amongst
the snails with painted shells,

a sand painting from Tunisia and a
barometer shaped like a pixie
from Bracklesham Bay.

"I'm awfully sorry," Miss
Johnson said to Jessica's granny.
"You're welcome to stay, but I'm
afraid Jessica hasn't quite
understood about 'Unusual Day'.
She was supposed to bring
something out of the ordinary.
Something the others might not
see every day."

22

Jessica's granny said she
understood and would come
back next week. She kissed
Jessica and left.

That afternoon all the other
children stood up one by one and
explained their unusual things.
Jessica wasn't paying attention.
She was cross. Even Reuben's

Australian hat and Katie's doll which could yodel the Austrian National Anthem didn't interest her. Jessica knew her granny would have been the most unusual of all.

Jessica had met other grannies. They cooked and sewed and slept through the news. Hers built walls, retiled the roof and spent one summer digging her own swimming pool. Other grannies knitted for a hobby.

Jessica's went windsurfing. Not all
the time. When there was no wind
she went roller-skating.

Jessica did perk up a bit at
Matthew's turn. He'd brought in
his sister's doll which someone

had fed real porridge. He was just
showing everyone that it now had
a black tummy under its dress
when Kristian noticed the smoke.

"I think there's a fire," said Kristian loudly.

"Kristian," said Miss Johnson, "please wait your turn. Matthew hasn't finished with his doll yet."

"Well, if there isn't a fire, then someone's having a barbecue in the playground."

Kristian was bored with unusual things and thought even the most ordinary of fires would be much more exciting.

"Shall I have a look?" said Jessica.

"Fire, fire!" Reuben and some of the other boys started chanting while Esme began beating time on her desk with a Russian doll.

"But it's my turn to speak!" bawled Phoebe, who was next after Matthew. "I've got a sand crab with a face like *Paddington Bear*." And she burst into tears.

The morning was not going as well as Miss Johnson had hoped. "Boys! Esme! Phoebe, you're too old for this kind of thing."

Just then Peter the caretaker appeared in the doorway.

"Miss Johnson, Blue Class," he said, "I don't want you to be alarmed. I'm afraid the house next door is on fire. The children are quite safe in here. I've called the fire brigade."

Down the road the children
could hear sirens coming closer.
Kristian and Jessica could not
sit for another moment. They
rushed to the window. Across the
playground they could see smoke
pouring out of the large Victorian

house next to the school. Soon all the children were gathered round the windows to see the fire engines arrive.

"Here comes one!" shouted Reuben as a giant red truck pulled up outside.

"And another!" cried Esme.

Soon three enormous fire engines filled the car park and firemen in blue uniforms and hard yellow hats swarmed outside the building. Hose-pipes and ladders appeared from everywhere.

"Look!" said Jessica. "It's Mrs Heathrington!"

Chapter Three

Everyone in Blue Class knew Mrs Heathrington. She waved to them every morning and once a week brought in biscuits for them all. She was very good at baking and although she was very old, she knew a surprising amount about the records of Lady Gaga.

In the very top window of the smoking building the children could just see the old lady. She

was calling down to the people
below. Smoke gushed all around
her and soon it was difficult to
see her properly.

The firemen quickly winched their ladder round to the window and one of them began to climb. For a short moment at the top of the ladder, the fireman disappeared altogether in the smoke. The children cheered as

he reappeared carrying Mrs
Heathrington on his shoulder.

"My word," said Miss Johnson,
still trying to get Phoebe to stop
crying.

Miss Johnson opened the class door out into the playground and waved to the firemen. "You can bring Mrs Heathrington in here if you like."

The children stood back as two firemen brought the old lady into the classroom. Mrs Heathrington had soot on her face and looked very tired. Jessica got her a chair.

Kristian offered her the rest of his
blackcurrant drink but she didn't
seem interested.

"My Bunsie, my Bunsie," Mrs
Heathrington whispered over
and over.

"You're all right," said Miss

44

Johnson soothingly. "You're all
right, Mrs Heathrington."

"My Bunsie, my Bunsie,"
the old woman kept repeating.

Miss Johnson patted her hand
and then took Phoebe off to
change her pants.

"Bunsie's her rabbit," said
Jessica knowledgeably. "Her
rabbit must still be in the house!"
"The rabbit, the rabbit!" the
whole of Blue Class began
shouting across to the firemen.
"Mrs Heathrington's rabbit is
still inside."

Through the haze, the children could see a fireman in his yellow helmet climbing back up the long ladder. The bright hat disappeared through the smoke and into the top window.

The children fell silent as they watched.

"Do you think Bunsie will be OK?" whispered Kristian.

"Absolutely," said Jessica, although she didn't feel sure.

They had to wait a long time. Longer than it took Jessica's

Uncle Charlie to explain why
sums are so simple. At last the
fireman reappeared in the window.

"Where's the rabbit?" said Esme.

"He hasn't got the rabbit," said
Katie.

"My Bunsie, my Bunsie," said
Mrs Heathrington.

No-one said a word. The
fireman climbed slowly down the
long ladder. At the bottom, he
turned and reached inside his
jacket. Suddenly a great cheer
went up from the class.

"It's in his jacket!" shouted
Kristian. "He's got it in his jacket."

From inside his heavy blue
coat, the fireman pulled out the
coughing rabbit. He held the
bewildered bunny up for the
children to see and they began

dancing and singing around Mrs
Heathrington.

"Bunsie's safe, Bunsie's safe!"

Chapter Four

"I'd better see if we can get the firemen some tea," said Miss Johnson, coming back in with Phoebe.

Soon the fire was out and just a little smoke lingered in the air.

The firemen began winding up
their hoses and Miss Johnson
called them in to have tea in
the hall. Their great boots made
muddy tracks across the wooden
floor but even Miss Walton, the
headmistress, didn't seem to mind.

"Miss Johnson, Granny wants a word," said Jessica to Miss Johnson who was handing out custard creams.

"Not just now, Jessica," said Miss Johnson. "I told you, Granny can come on 'Family Day'."

"But she wants to know if
Blue Class can look after Bunsie
while Mrs Heathrington stays
with her sister."

Miss Johnson was confused.

Jessica led her over to the fireman who had rescued Bunsie. Miss Johnson looked carefully at the uniformed officer. The fireman took off his hat. Except he wasn't a 'he' at all. Standing in front of

Miss Johnson, in a dirty fireman's uniform and with a smudged face, was Jessica's granny.

"You're a . . . I mean you . . ." Miss Johnson could hardly speak. "You went up the ladder . . . and . . . Mrs Heathrington . . . your shoulder . . ."

Miss Johnson had to sit down.
It was Jessica's granny who had
rescued Mrs Heathrington and
Jessica's granny who had gone
back for the rabbit. Jessica's
granny was the fireman.

"I'm sorry, Jessica," said Miss
Johnson. "I see why you wanted
your granny here on 'Unusual
Day'. It really is most unusual to
have a granny who is a fireman."

"Oh, that isn't why I brought
her," said Jessica, who had never
thought of Granny's job as
different. "I think Granny's

unusual because she can spin plates. Mum says she just wishes Granny wouldn't do it with food still on them!"

THE END